THE UNICORN WISHES
UNITY
UNICORN OF THE MEADOW

Published in the UK in 2021 by Potter Press

Second Edition

This book is a work of fiction, any resemblance
to names, place and characters, living or dead, is
purely coincidental.

Paperback ISBN 978-1-8383344-3-7
.epub eBook 978-1-8383344-1-3
.mobi eBook ISBN 978-1-8383344-2-0

Cover design and typeset by SpiffingCovers

THE UNICORN WISHES
UNITY
UNICORN OF THE MEADOW

NICOLA FRANCESCA

For Satya

"Well, now that we have seen each other," said the unicorn,

"if you'll believe in me, I'll believe in you..."

From
THROUGH THE LOOKING-GLASS
by
LEWIS CARROLL

THE LEGEND OF THE UNICORNS

For thousands of years,
in stories and songs,
Unicorns have been righting wrongs.
They're mythical creatures,
gentle and wise,
Who only have love and peace
on their minds.
They have horns on their foreheads and,
as you may know,
They bring joy and happiness
wherever they go.

The Arrival of the Unicorns

Long ago and far away,
out in the darkness of space,
Celeste, the unicorn mother,
created the unicorn race.
Her heart sent out a billion stars,
each as bright as the brightest sun,
And all around the universe
they became unicorns, every one.

Celeste wanted every galaxy
to be filled with their love,
And the unicorns were her messengers,
arriving from above.
Each had a birth-star
that sparkled with light,
And had the power to grant wishes
to make everything all right.

Celeste, the unicorn mother, is from ancient times. She is as wise as can be, with eyes the colour of the bluest ocean. She is sparkling white from her mane to her tail, and her heart is as pure as mountain air.

Unity, the Unicorn of the Meadow, is the eldest of the unicorn family and lives in Sparkle Meadow. She loves to dance, and has silver sparkles in her mane that look like daisies shining with morning dew. Sometimes she gets very excitable and a bit bossy, but she never wishes harm on anyone. She loves all creatures of Earth.

Seraphina, the Unicorn of the Sky, is the softest of pinks, with huge wings to carry her through the air. She can sometimes be grumpy, but not for long. She lives high in the clouds, and likes to choose particularly fluffy clouds to sleep and dream on as they drift in the blue skies.

Freya, the Unicorn of the Forest, has a deep golden nose and a light golden mane and tail. She is very sensible and always knows what to do in a crisis. She loves her life in Dapple Woods, where she can talk to the scurrying insects and listen to the breeze in the trees.

Marina, the Unicorn of the Sea, is a beautiful glistening aquamarine colour that looks like the sun's rays bouncing off the crest of an ocean wave. She lives beneath the sea in White Sands Bay and spends her days diving with the dolphins and learning their secret language. But she also likes to be alone, watching the sunlight through the water, or lying on the white sand listening to the waves.

The Sky Above the Realm

Army of Trees

White Sands Bay

The Prickly Wasteland

Muddy Hole

Chapter One
Where is Prudence?

Unity woke up to see bright sunshine streaming in through her bedroom window. It was going to be another lovely summer's day.

Like the other young unicorns, Unity had a bright birth-star on her body. This was a magical birthmark that gave the unicorns the power to grant wishes – but only one a day.

"I can't wait to go and find Prudence, so we can dance some more," she said as she stretched and got to her feet.

Prudence was a gorgeous butterfly who

lived in Sparkle Meadow with Unity. She had scarlet wings and a body of shimmering crimson. She was fragile and sweet.

Unity and Prudence were best friends who saw each other every day. They loved to dance together to the songs of the birds and the music of the wind. But their favourite place was near the waterfall, where the sound of the water was the most beautiful music of all.

After eating her breakfast, washing her face and cleaning her teeth, Unity galloped out to find Prudence.

"I wish I could call her Pru, but she doesn't like it. I'll just call her that to myself instead." Unity sighed.

The little waterfall was where Unity and Prudence had danced yesterday, so Unity went there first.

"I expect she's waiting for me, fluttering above the water like a tiny scarlet and crimson rainbow," she said. But her special friend was not there. Unity frowned. "I'll try the songbirds' rock instead."

The songbirds were singing loud and clear, but nobody was dancing to their sweet music. Where was Prudence?

"Could she be in the tiny wood, where the wind sings through the trees?" she wondered. She galloped over to the tiny wood. "No sign of her..." she said. "Oh, where *is* she?"

Unity wandered around all morning looking for Prudence, but she was nowhere to be found.

"Something's wrong," she said to herself. "Pru has never gone missing like this before. I hope she's all right..."

"She's fine," said one of the songbirds passing overhead. "I saw her just now, flying away from the meadow."

Unity couldn't believe her ears. "Why

was she flying away?" she gasped.

Then Unity remembered what had happened yesterday. She and Prudence had been practicing a new dance routine. It had been great fun and they'd almost made it perfect.

"One more time," Unity had said.

"Not today," her friend had replied. "My wings are tired and I want to sit in the sun to rest them."

"Oh, come on, Pru. Just one more dance. Please? **Pretty** please?" Unity begged.

"Oh, all right then," Prudence agreed wearily. "But stop calling me Pru! I don't like it. My name is Pru**dence**!"

By the end of the last dance, the delicate butterfly had been quite worn out.

"I'm going home now," she had called, using her last bit of energy to lift herself into the air.

"See you tomorrow!" Unity called back, but Prudence hadn't answered her.

Now the little unicorn knew what was wrong.

"I was mean and bossy and I've upset her," she sobbed, tears splashing down from her lovely round eyes. "She's flown away because she doesn't want to be my friend any more. We'll never dance together again!"

Chapter Two
Searching the Realm

Unity sat down and cried some more, but then she jumped up.

"It's no use sitting here feeling sorry for myself!" she exclaimed. "I must carry on looking for Pru. Maybe the other unicorns will know where she is."

With new hope in her heart, Unity galloped off to find her sister, Seraphina, the Unicorn of the Sky. She was fast asleep on a white cloud that was floating overhead.

"Wake up, Seraphina," Unity called up to her pretty pink sister. "I've got something important to ask you!"

Seraphina woke with a start. "I was dreaming about being on a white sandy beach beside a clear blue sea," she said, sounding a bit cross. "I was sunbathing. It was lovely…"

"Sorry," said Unity.

"It doesn't matter, I'm awake now," Seraphina sighed, unfolding her beautiful wings and gliding down with her long white tail flowing behind her. She landed with a gentle bump in front of her sister. "Okay, then. What's up?"

Unity told her that Prudence was missing, but didn't tell her why the butterfly had flown away. Unity was ashamed of being unkind to her little friend and didn't want anybody to know about it until she'd made everything better again.

"Sorry, Unity, I'm afraid I haven't seen her," said Seraphina, shaking her long

white mane from side to side. "Why don't you ask Freya? She might know."

Their sister Freya was the Unicorn of the Forest. She lived in Dapple Woods in another part of the Unicorn Realm. Unity set off at a gallop to get there as fast as she could.

As she entered the wood, she tripped over a log and fell forwards, and her horn hit a tree trunk and got stuck.

"HELP! I'm stuck!" she yelled. "Freya, are you there? Help me!"

"Don't panic, Unity," Freya called, hearing her sister. "I'm coming!"

Unity's horn was stuck fast, but her woodland sister knew what to do.

"Turn your head carefully from side to side," she said calmly, "and it will come loose."

"Are you sure?" Unity asked. "I don't want it to snap off. That would hurt, and unicorn horns take ages to grow back."

"Stop panicking," Freya said, giving her sister a soothing nudge with her soft golden nose. "If I had a wild strawberry for every time I got my horn stuck in a tree, I'd be a very happy bunny."

"But you're not a bunny, you're a unicorn..."

"Oh, get on with it, silly! Wiggle your head like I told you."

Freya's advice was good and Unity's horn was soon free. It wasn't damaged and it didn't hurt, so all was well.

"Anyway, to what do I owe your visit?" Freya asked, the breeze making the trees rustle and her light golden mane ruffle.

"I can't find my best friend Pru..." Unity explained, "and we were supposed to be dancing together today. Have you seen her, Freya? If she's here, she's a long way from home and might be rather scared."

"I'm afraid I haven't, dear," Freya
sighed. "There are many pretty butterflies
in this wood, but none of them look like
your special friend. Try asking Marina."

With a nod of her head, Unity thanked
Freya and galloped off to White Sands
Bay. This was where Marina lived, and it
was even further from Sparkle Meadow
than Dapple Woods. But her sister wasn't
there on the sand, so Unity stood on the
shoreline and called her name over and
over again.

At last a shape appeared from under
the water and the beautiful blue of her
sister Marina, the Unicorn of the Sea,
came splashing ashore.

Unity wasted no time asking her if she
had seen Prudence.

Marina shook her long wave-like
mane, sprinkling water all over Unity.

Usually this would have made Unity

laugh, but she was far too worried to find it funny. She had spent a lot of the day travelling around the realm, and her little friend was still missing.

"What am I going to do, Marina?" she wailed, tears filling her eyes again. "You're the last person I've visited. There's nobody else to ask."

"Are you talking about Prudence, the butterfly from Sparkle Meadow?" said a voice nearby.

"If you are," added a second voice, that sounded almost exactly the same as the first, "we saw her earlier."

Two brown fox cubs had come down to the beach to play. They liked chasing along the sands and playing hide-and-seek amongst the rocks. They didn't really know very much about unicorns, but they'd heard from their elders that they were magical creatures from the old, old days, who appeared in stories in places called India and China and Greece.

"Where?" Unity asked eagerly. "Where did you see my friend?"

"Over there," replied the first cub, pointing to some wild countryside in the distance.

"She was being carried along by the wind," said the second, his orange-yellow eyes shining.

This part of the Unicorn Realm was called the Prickly Wasteland, and Unity had never been there before.

"You must go," Marina said, "if you want to find your friend."

"But I don't want to go alone," Unity said.

Marina smiled at her sister, and Unity knew she must be brave, so she thanked the two fox cubs, who gambolled away, rolling over each other as they ran, and made her way to the edge of the Prickly Wasteland.

Chapter Three
Searching in the Prickly Wasteland

Unity could see why this area of the realm was called 'prickly'. There were spiky trees and bushes with thorns. The ground was bumpy and the wind was much stronger than the woodland breeze she was used to, blowing across the wasteland in big gusts.

"I d-don't like it here," Unity said with a shudder.

She really wanted to turn away and go back home, but knew she couldn't do that. It would mean not finding Prudence, and that would be much meaner than making her dance when she didn't want to.

"I must go on," she said firmly, and marched boldly into the wilderness.

At first it was all right. There was a path that other travellers had taken through the bushes, and it was wide enough for Unity to walk along safely. Further on, though, the path became narrower and then ran out altogether, and Unity had no choice but to squeeze through all the scratchy thorns and prickles.

"Ouch!" she cried as she went along. "Ouch! Ouch!"

And then her silvery mane got caught on a spiky branch, and as she tugged and pulled she remembered her sister Freya's calm words when her horn had been stuck in the tree.

"Don't panic," she said, and carefully moved her head this way and that until she was free. She bravely kept going until

she reached some open ground. At last she was free of the spiky, nasty brambles!

"Where are you, Pru?" Unity called. And then, remembering that her friend didn't like to be called Pru, she shouted, "Prudence, I'm here! It's your friend Unity, and I'm coming to find you, and I won't stop until I do!"

Glad to have left the prickles behind, Unity criss-crossed the wide-open space calling out her friend's name as loudly as she could; but the only reply was the howling and moaning of the wind.

"I *do* hope I find Pru soon," Unity whispered, her voice sore from calling, and her legs tired from all the galloping and trotting and walking... And then SPLASH! her foot went down a hole!

She had been so busy looking up to see if she could see Prudence that she hadn't noticed the holes all over the open plain. Long green weeds had grown over the top of them, and they looked like patches of grass instead of holes. She should have been paying attention!

"Help!" she yelled. It was all squelchy in the hole, and she didn't like it.

Feeling her foot sliding around in the horrid wet mud, Unity knew she had to do something, and leaned backwards and pulled with all her might. Slowly... slowly...her foot started to move, and then SCHLURP! it came out in a rush, making her stumble backwards.

"No harm done," she muttered, trying to shake the mud off.

She really didn't like this place, and looked about, wondering where to search next. On the edge of the open space stood some trees in lines, like rows of soldiers. All the trees looked the same, not very tall but thin, with no leaves on their branches, but one caught Unity's eye because it had a colourful scarf stuck on it, flapping in the wind like a flag.

"That's *my* scarf!" she gasped in

amazement. "How on earth did it get here?" She trotted over. "I must have left it outside my house and it's blown all the way here, just like Pru... Maybe it's a sign? Maybe she's near here and I'm going to find her at last!"

Using the scarf as a starting point, she went left and right, up and down, hoping to find her friend somewhere amongst the lines of trees. She'd been searching nearly all day now and she was starting to feel very tired indeed, but knew she had to keep going.

"Maybe she's this way. I haven't looked over here before," she said, wandering off to the left.

But she had! She was back at the tree with the scarf!

"I've gone right round in a circle!" she cried. "Oh no! I'm never going to find her!"

Unity tried to stop herself from crying again. She'd done enough of that already. But she felt really unhappy now, because she'd been searching in this horrid place for *sooooo* long and had **still** not managed to find Prudence. What was she going to do? She slumped down into the spiky grass.

She was trying to find the strength to carry on when she heard a buzzing noise above her head. Looking up, she saw a large group of bumblebees coming towards her. She knew they were friendly because they all had smiling faces. They hovered in front of her, each one talking to her in turn...

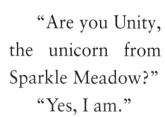

"Are you Unity, the unicorn from Sparkle Meadow?"

"Yes, I am."

"We heard you

23

were here. You're looking for your lost butterfly friend, I believe?"

"Yes, that's right."

"We know where she is."

"You do? Oh, that's wonderful!"

"Come on, follow us. We'll take you to her now."

The bumblebees knew all about unicorns, as they often heard the flowers chatting about them as they flitted to and fro collecting pollen. One of their most favourite flowers, the tall, yellow goldenrod, said that unicorns could heal wounds, like they could, but with a single touch of their beautiful spiral horn. The bumblebees knew when a unicorn was in trouble, because it stopped happily trotting about helping everybody else and instead looked sad and lonely, like Unity did.

"Come on," they said. "You can do this."

Tired, but with joy in her heart, Unity got to her feet and followed the bumblebees. Other members of the swarm joined in from all sides, until they looked like a black and yellow buzzing cloud moving through the air.

"Nearly there, Unity," called the last bumblebee in the cloud, turning around to give her a big grin.

When the swarm reached the edge

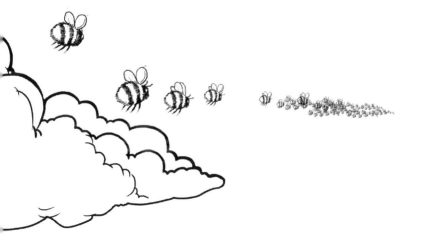

of the woods with the thin trees, the cloud changed shape. Unity watched in amazement as it swept upwards and turned into a big buzzing arrow, pointing downwards.

"SHE'S HERE!" all the bumblebees shouted together.

Unity galloped forwards like a racehorse.

"I can't believe it," she puffed. "I'm so happy!"

The swarming cloud changed shape again and flew away in a curved line, like aeroplanes doing a display.

"Glad we could help you," called the

leading bee. "We have to buzz off now and make some more honey."

Unity was so relieved, but then she stopped short.

Prudence was here, but she was in trouble...

Chapter Four
A Sticky Situation

Her beautiful, butterfly friend was caught on a big spider's web that stretched between two trees.

"Unity?" Prudence said, her voice weak.

"How did this happen?" Unity gasped. "And why did you come this far?"

"I flew to the end of the meadow, because I didn't want to play with you today, because you were bossy and made me dance when I was tired," Prudence said. "Then a gust of wind caught me and blew me all the way here. I've been stuck

in this web ever since."

"I'm so sorry–" Unity began.

"Let's talk later," Prudence interrupted. "Please could you set me free, and sort of right now."

There was nothing Unity wanted to do more than free her friend, but she wasn't sure how to do it. She stood and thought for a moment.

"I know," she then said. "I'll carefully scrape the web away with my foot."

Unicorns have hooves on their feet just like horses, but they're quite big and this wasn't the best idea. Unity lifted her foot and tried to scrape the web but RIP! OOPS! she only managed to tear a hole in the web, and nearly hit Prudence on the head as well!

"Think again, please," said the little butterfly.

"Shall I try using my horn? That's

much thinner and lighter," she said brightly. "You'll be free in no time."

Unity lowered her horn under the web and started to pull the strands away. They were very sticky, and soon she had a big blob, like candy floss, on her face!

"You *do* look funny," Prudence giggled, "but I'm still stuck!"

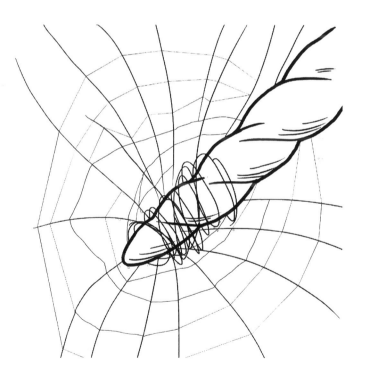

Unity didn't know what to do next. She had travelled all over the Unicorn Realm and found her best friend, at last, but they still couldn't go home together. It was starting to get really dark now. And what if the spider showed up to check Prudence was still there? She didn't want them to spend the night in this wilderness. She had to think of something.

Then something made Unity look up. What was that in the sky? She looked again. It was a shooting star, and it glittered and sparkled as it sped across the darkness. Celeste, her unicorn mother, was sending a reminder to her child!

Unity started laughing. Why hadn't she remembered? "Of course!" she said. "I can use my birth-star!"

"What birth-star?" Prudence asked.

"My birth-star, it grants wishes," Unity said, showing it to Prudence.

"Just hurry!" Prudence said, hoping that what Unity had said was true.

But Unity couldn't remember what to say to make her birth-star work. She hadn't used it since Mother Celeste had explained to all of her daughters how to grant a wish. She wandered away from the web to think very carefully.

"Don't leave me!" Prudence called in an anxious voice.

"I won't go far," Unity replied, looking over her shoulder and smiling. "And I'll be back in a moment, I promise."

Closing her eyes, she thought hard... And then it all came back in a flash.

"I have to say the rhyme we learned, and then make one up of my own, about the wish, and then the wish will work!"

she murmured to herself.

"**Please** hurry up, Unity!" urged Prudence.

"Coming!"

Unity hurried back and stood in front of the giant cobweb.

She began to recite the rhyme:

"Unicorns bring love and peace,
They make joy and hope increase.
Whatever's wrong can be made fine,
By granting this single wish of mine."

"Nothing's happened," Prudence whispered. She was cold now, and tired of being trapped.

Unity then made up her own rhyme:

"My best friend Pru is very dear,
But sadly she's a prisoner here.
My wish is that she could be free,
So she can come home with me."

When the second rhyme finished, the big silver star on Unity's body began to

glow. Then a stream of tiny sparkling stars shot out, and they fizzed and popped as they touched the web. Instantly, it began to disappear and was completely gone in a matter of seconds.

"I'm free! I'm free!" whooped Prudence, flapping her wings with delight.

The little butterfly flew round in a circle, with Unity chasing after her. They both felt their hearts would burst with joy.

Then Prudence stopped and hovered in the air, casting her eyes upwards.

"Look how dark it is, Unity," she said. "We should leave now or we'll both get lost!"

The two friends need not have worried. As if Unity's mother had heard them, the full moon came out from behind a cloud, big and round and really bright. It lit up the ground below like a floodlight, and they carefully started to make their way out of the Prickly Wasteland, back through the lines of trees standing like soldiers, back across the open plain with the muddy holes, and into the prickly, spiky bushes to the path.

"I can see our meadow," called Prudence, fluttering high in the air. But there was still a long way to go, and Prudence's wings had started to ache again. "I don't think I can fly much more," she said.

"Come down and land on me. I'll give you a ride. I know the way from here,"

Unity said, and Prudence fluttered down to ride on the end of Unity's horn.

"It feels a bit like flying," Prudence said, "but bumpier."

"I'll walk carefully," Unity said, smiling. "We'll be home soon."

Chapter Five
A Gift of Honey

The next day, after a good long sleep, Unity and Prudence met up in the meadow.

"Time for me to talk," said Unity.

"I'm listening," said Prudence.

Unity said she was very sorry for being mean and bossy and making Prudence unhappy. She promised never to do it again, and to listen when her friend said she was tired. She said she hoped they could still be the best of friends.

"Thank you for saying sorry," Prudence answered, fluttering her beautiful crimson wings. "You came all that way to rescue me. That was very brave of you. I think you've shown you're a very special friend so, yes, we can still be the best of friends."

Tears started to trickle down Unity's face again, but this time they were happy tears. "Thank you, Prudence," she said.

Now they were friends again, Prudence wondered what they could do together on this lovely sunny morning.

"There's only one thing we can do," Unity laughed.

"What's that?"

"Dance!"

"Of course!" cried Prudence. "Why didn't I think of that?"

To the tinkling music of the waterfall, the two of them practiced their new routine again, moving in harmony with each other and not caring that it wasn't perfect.

"I wish we could show someone," sighed Prudence.

"Me too," Unity agreed.

Then some figures appeared in the distance, from three different directions.

"Coo-eee!" they called together.

It was Unity's sisters, Seraphina, Freya and Marina. They had come to see if she had found her lost friend. When they saw the two of them dancing together in the sunshine, they all broke into a gallop and came to watch the performance; and when it had finished, they shook their manes and pawed the ground with their hooves, which was the unicorn way of clapping.

"That was amazing!" Freya said.

"I'd quite like to join in myself," Marina added.

"Then what are we waiting for?" cried Seraphina, nodding at the waterfall. "The music's still playing. Let's dance!"

Soon all four of the star-born unicorns were laughing and dancing together, and Prudence flitted around, helping them with the steps.

When they had finished, everyone felt hot and tired, and they had a long drink from the pool below the waterfall. Then they lay down on the soft green grass to rest.

"What's that buzzing noise ?" Marina asked, raising her head.

"No idea," Freya answered.

"Me neither," agreed Seraphina.

Unity knew what it was. She jumped up. "It's my new friends, the bumblebees.

They've come to visit too... And wow! Look what they've brought with them!"

It was a big honeycomb, dripping with clear golden honey.

The bumblebees put down the honeycomb, and started to fly away, curving in big arcs and spirals.

"Aren't you going to stay? Everyone loves eating honey!" Unity called.

"Not us," replied one of the bees. "We like *making* honey!"

"And we're off to collect pollen from the meadow flowers so we can make some more," explained another.

The honey tasted delicious, but it was very sticky and the unicorn sisters got into a terrible mess!

"My mane's stuck to yours," Freya said to Seraphina.

"And I've got honey on my foot!" groaned Marina.

Prudence stayed well clear, fluttering around high above them all. "I've had quite enough of sticky things, thank you very much!" she laughed.

A good wash in the pool made everyone clean again, and then they stood drying in the sunshine.

"Time we were going," said Marina, planting a big kiss on Unity's nose.

Freya and Seraphina did the same, before they all set off to their homes in the Unicorn Realm.

Unity and Prudence waved goodbye and sat down together by the waterfall.

"It's my turn now to grant *you* a wish," said the butterfly.

Unity looked puzzled. "How?" she asked. "You don't have a birth-star."

"I don't need a birth-star!"

"Okay, then... But how do you know what I want to wish?"

Prudence gave a huge smile. "I know exactly what your wish is, and your wish is granted. From now on, you can call me Pru…"

Unity's sisters
have their own stories too...

SERAPHINA,
THE UNICORN OF THE SKY

Seraphina wants to carry out her unicorn
duty of bringing happiness to others, but
doesn't feel she can do it. Then a mistake
with her daily wish sends her on a daring
adventure that puts her in great danger.
Will this result in the little flying unicorn
gaining her confidence?

*A story full of action, excitement and joy
that will delight young readers aged five
and over.*

Freya,
the Unicorn of the Forest

Freya is tired of Dapple Wood and wishes she lived somewhere else in the Unicorn Realm. So Tayo, her wise old fox friend, shows her some wonders of the forest she has never seen. She goes on to discover more herself, but what's in this secret hidden world? *A unicorn adventure full of magic, mystery and enchantment – perfect for young readers.*

Marina,
the Unicorn of the Sea

Despite being Unicorn of the Sea, Marina doesn't feel she belongs because she looks so different from everyone else. Not wanting to be seen anymore, she sets off with her best friend Bottle, the baby dolphin, to find a cave in which to hide away. It's a sad plan...but will the creatures she meets and the adventures she has with them on the way make her change her mind?

A funny and action-packed story about a special young unicorn guaranteed to delight young readers.

Why not collect them all?

Dear Reader

Thank you for reading Unity: Unicorn of the Meadow. If you enjoyed this book please consider leaving a star rating or review online.

Your feedback is important, and will help other readers to find the book and decide whether to read it, too.

Printed in Great Britain
by Amazon

17834156R00041